Sheep on the Run!

by Alice Hemming
illustrated by David Creighton-Pester

Farmer Green is ill. He is in bed.

"I cannot feed the sheep and pigs!"

says Farmer Green.

"I will feed them for you," says Lee.

"Good! But you must shut
the sheep and pigs in the pens,"
says Farmer Green.

Lee feeds the sheep.

The sheep eat.

But then...

Lee forgets to shut the pen!

The sheep are on the run.

Lee feeds the pigs. The pigs eat.

But then Lee sees...

...A sheep in the pig pen.

Oink!

Then Lee sees... a sheep in the mud.

Splat!

And then Lee sees...

three sheep in the jeep.

Beep, beep!

Lee shuts the sheep back in the pen.

Then Lee sets off to see Farmer Green.

"Did you shut the pen?"

says Farmer Green.

"Yes," says Lee.

"All the sheep are in the pen."

But no! Look at this sheep...

...asleep.

Quiz

1. Why can Farmer Green not feed the sheep?
a) He is in the jeep
b) He is ill
c) He is asleep

2. What does Lee forget to do?
a) Feed the pigs
b) See Farmer Green
c) Shut the pen

3. Where does Lee see the sheep?
a) In the pig pen
b) In a tractor
c) In a rocket

4. What noise does the Jeep make?
a) Honk, Honk!
b) Beep, Beep!
c) Boom, Boom!

5. Where is the last sheep?
a) In Farmer Green's bed
b) In the shed
c) On the sofa

Turn over for answers

Book Bands for Guided Reading

The Institute of Education book banding system is a scale of colours that reflects the various levels of reading difficulty. The bands are assigned by taking into account the content, the language style, the layout and phonics.

Maverick Early Readers are a bright, attractive range of books covering the pink to purple bands. All of these books have been book banded for guided reading to the industry standard and edited by a leading educational consultant.

For more titles visit:
www.maverickbooks.co.uk/early-readers

 Pink

 Red

 Yellow

 Blue

 Green

 Orange

 Turquoise

 Purple

 Book Band Yellow

Little Fish and Big Fish	978-1-84886-292-0
Sheep on the Run	978-1-84886-291-3
The Dog and the Fox	978-1-84886-293-7
Can I Have My Ball Back?	978-1-84886-252-4
Izzy! Wizzy!	978-1-84886-253-1

Quiz Answers: 1b, 2c, 3a, 4b, 5a